BRIAN MEUNIER

*

ILLUSTRATED BY

PERKY EDGERTON

*

DUTTON
CHILDREN'S
BOOKS

BRAVO, TAVO!

DUTTON CHILDREN'S BOOKS

A division of Penguin Young Readers Group

Published by the Penguin Group • Penguin Group (USA) Inc., 375 Hudson Street, New York, New York 10014, U.S.A. • Penguin Group (Canada), 90 Eglinton Avenue East, Suite 700, Toronto, Ontario, Canada M4P 2Y3 (a division of Pearson Penguin Canada Inc.) • Penguin Books Ltd, 80 Strand, London WC2R 0RL, England • Penguin Ireland, 25 St Stephen's Green, Dublin 2, Ireland (a division of Penguin Books Ltd) • Penguin Group (Australia), 250 Camberwell Road, Camberwell, Victoria 3124, Australia (a division of Pearson Australia Group Pty Ltd) • Penguin Books India Pvt Ltd, 11 Community Centre, Panchsheel Park, New Delhi - 110 017, India • Penguin Group (NZ), Cnr Airborne and Rosedale Roads, Albany, Auckland 1310, New Zealand (a division of Pearson New Zealand Ltd) • Penguin Books (South Africa) (Pty) Ltd, 24 Sturdee Avenue, Rosebank, Johannesburg 2196, South Africa • Penguin Books Ltd, Registered Offices: 80 Strand, London WC2R 0RL, England

Library of Congress Cataloging-in-Publication Data

Meunier, Brian.

Bravo, Tavo! / by Brian Meunier ; illustrated by Perky Edgerton. — 1st. ed.

p. cm.

Summary: Tavo dreams of nothing but being a famous basketball star—and getting new shoes so that he can practice better—but his village in Mexico faces a serious drought, and Tavo and his father must work to convince the other people that the old way of irrigation will save their crops.

ISBN 978-0-525-47478-4 (hardcover)

［1. Droughts—Fiction. 2. Irrigation—Fiction. 3. Agriculture—Fiction. 4. Basketball—Fiction. 5. Shoes—Fiction. 6. Mexico—Fiction.］

I. Edgerton, Perky, ill. II. Title.

PZ7.M56792Bra 2007 ［E］—dc22 2006024466

Published in the United States by Dutton Children's Books,
a division of Penguin Young Readers Group
345 Hudson Street, New York, New York 10014
www.penguingroup.com/youngreaders

Designed by Heather Wood

Manufactured in China • First Edition

10 9 8 7 6 5 4 3 2 1

For Pepere, Dede, and Baba

B.A.M. & P.E.

Dribble-*flip*, dribble-*boing*...

The ball bounced off the hoop. Tavo had missed again.

   He bent down to fix the duct tape flapping around his patched sneakers. The tape held the soles to what remained of the canvas tops. But Tavo wasn't easily discouraged. He was excited, for he had the whole summer to practice before the regular basketball season started.

   Tavo had seen the NBA games on the new satellite TV at the village store, and he wanted to play ball like one of those big American players. He imagined that one day he, too, would have a great basketball name. A name like Air or Magic.

   But for now, he was just Tavo. Gustavo the second . . . named after his father.

"If only I had new sneakers," Tavo said to himself as he tucked the ball under his arm and started up the path toward home. "Then I'd play better."

The ground crunched beneath his shoes, leaving trails of dust. The mountainside stretched before him, a patchwork of plowed fields separated by the remnants of ancient irrigation ditches called *zanjas*. It reminded him of the quilt on his bed, but in shades of brown. Tavo looked down at his frayed sneakers and kicked at the parched earth.

"If only I had new sneakers," he muttered again.

When he reached home, Tavo found his father poking around the old *zanja*, the ancient irrigation ditch, which ran along the edge of their field. Gustavo was always tinkering with something. Today he was putting up yet another scarecrow.

"Papa . . . look. Look at my sneakers. They are turning into sandals! I bet you can't fix them anymore," said Tavo.

"Tavo, I've told you this already," Gustavo replied wearily. "We can't afford new sneakers right now. Not until the rains come."

Sure, Tavo thought in frustration. *And* then . . . *I'll have to wait for the corn to grow.* Then, *to dry on the stalk.* Then, *to be harvested.* Then, *to be brought to the* molino *to be ground into flour.* Then, *to be sold in the market. The basketball season will be over by* then!

Tavo looked up at the sky as some dark thunderclouds rumbled with the promise of rain. One cloud slipped through the peaks and drifted out over the valley.

The two Gustavos watched silently as the cloud broke apart in the blazing sun, like a bursting piñata.

"Hopeless!" Gustavo said, throwing up his hands in exasperation. "There is only one thing left to do. I have a plan, and I'm going to present it at the meeting tonight."

The villagers had been called to an emergency meeting to discuss the drought. As the two Gustavos neared the village square, they could hear that the meeting had already begun. To Tavo's surprise, his father marched right up to the front and faced the crowd.

"We cannot wait for the rains to begin," he said. "Our ancestors knew the solution. The solution is in the *zanjas*! We must dig them up again, up into the mountains until we reach the ancient source of the water!"

"Gustavo," the mayor said, pausing for effect. "Go talk to your scarecrows!" The crowd burst into laughter. "If the *zanjas* worked so well in the past, why did our ancestors stop using them?" The mayor puffed up his chest and poked his finger in the air. "We must move forward, not backward!"

Gustavo abruptly turned and walked out. Tavo ran after him, his back burning with embarrassment.

Early the next morning, Tavo awoke with a start. His father was shaking his shoulder.

"Tavo, wake up."

Tavo rubbed his eyes and protested. "It is still dark outside!"

"Get up, Tavo. We have a lot of work to do."

"But Papa, I have practice today."

Gustavo handed Tavo a shovel. "Son, basketball comes later."

The two Gustavos started work at the edge of their field. All day long they shoveled out the silt that had filled in the ancient *zanja*. When night finally came, Tavo slumped into bed, every bone in his body aching.

They began all over again the next morning. Digging and digging and digging some more. Hours turned into days. Days turned into weeks as father and son slowly worked their way up the mountain.

There was one house high up in the mountain. It belonged to an old widow. Tavo had heard strange stories about her.

"Is it true what they say about her, that she is a *bruja*, a witch?" he asked his father nervously.

"Tavo," his father laughed. "Don't believe everything you hear. Señora Rosa is just a widow. People are always suspicious of anyone who is different."

"Señora Rosa?" Gustavo called out.

There was no answer, but in the yard they saw a patchwork quilt draped over a chair. A needle dangling from a silver thread swayed in the air.

As they left, Gustavo carved a channel to connect Señora Rosa's small garden to the main *zanja*. He turned toward Tavo with a mischievous smile. "Even witches need water."

Higher and higher, they continued to dig. Weeks passed this way, and Tavo's muscles no longer ached from the hard work. One day, the two Gustavos worked their way up into a shadowy ravine near the top of the mountain. Under their feet the ground was soggy and green.

"We did it, Tavo! We found the spring!" Gustavo cried.

With triumph they cleared away the debris, and the water bubbled forth down the arid mountainside! Jubilant, they danced in its wake.

Down . . . down . . . down . . . splashing along.

Down . . . down . . . down . . . until the water reached their thirsty field.

As they whooped and hollered, Tavo felt the cool mud squishing between his toes. In his excitement, Tavo's ragged sneakers had slipped off his feet. And now they were lost somewhere in the muddy waters.

Without sneakers, Tavo could no longer practice with the team. Instead, he practiced his shots using an old barrel hoop that his father had nailed to a tree in their yard.

Even so, Tavo continued to go down to the village to watch his teammates practice. But he often found himself gazing up at the mountainside, at the one patch of green in that blanket of brown— his father's field.

If I can see it, they can, too. But why aren't people talking about this? Tavo puzzled. And then it dawned on him. Maybe they were just too proud to admit that Gustavo's idea had been a good one.

All of a sudden, Tavo had his own good idea.

The next morning Tavo got up early and walked toward their field, a machete in hand. At the edge of the field, he stopped and stared in amazement. There in front of him were his missing sneakers!

The duct tape was gone, but so were the holes. His sneakers had been beautifully patched! He recognized the fabric and the silver thread.

"Señora Rosa!" he whispered aloud. He laced the sneakers on. And his feet began to tingle.

Tavo grabbed a cornstalk and cut it close to the ground. Then he raced down the mountain path, straight to the mayor's house. With the magic sneakers on his feet, he felt as if he could fly.

Though it was still early, Tavo eagerly knocked on the door. The mayor opened it, blinking sleepily in the morning light.

Tavo raised the stalk high. But he didn't say anything.

Then the mayor let out a sigh, his face softening.

"Yes, Tavo . . . yes. I see it. I believe it's time we all see your father's field."

For the next several weeks, Gustavo was much in demand helping
the other villagers connect their own fields to the main *zanja*. And
Tavo rejoined his teammates on the basketball court for the first game
of the season.

From midcourt, Tavo could see his father, sitting in a place of honor
next to the mayor.

Then the game began.

And what a game it was! One minute, Tavo's team was ahead, and the next minute, behind. At the end, the game was tied. It went into overtime. Then the ball was in Tavo's hands.

He planted himself, and crouched. He felt the tingling sensation in his feet shoot upward, through the muscles of his arms made so strong from shoveling. The ball soared toward the basket.

Sw-o-o-o-sh!

The villagers went wild.

"Tavo, Tavo! Bravo, Tavo!" They chanted in unison.

And he liked the sound of it. Tavo was a great basketball name!

It was late by the time the two Gustavos started up the mountain toward home.

Gustavo looked over the moonlit fields high with corn. He stopped and put his hands on Tavo's shoulders.

"Son, it's time for new sneakers. What do you think?"

Tavo wiggled his toes. They still tingled with magic energy.

"No, Papa, these will do."